$13.95
383     Skurzynski,
SKU         Here comes the
        mail

| DATE DUE | BORROWER'S NAME | ROOM NUMBER |
|---|---|---|

$13.95
383     Skurzynski, Gloria
SKU         Here comes the
        mail

## DATE DUE

| | | | |
|---|---|---|---|
| MAR 1 6 1993 | | | |
| MAY 0 1 | | | |
| | | | |
| | | | |
| | | | |
| | | | |
| | | | |
| | | | |
| | | | |
| | | | |
| | | | |
| | | | |
| | | | |
| | | | |
| | | | |
| GAYLORD | | | PRINTED IN U.S.A. |

BRADBURY PRESS • *New York*

Maxwell Macmillan Canada *Toronto*

Maxwell Macmillan International

*New York* • *Oxford* • *Singapore* • *Sydney*

# *Here Comes the Mail*

## by Gloria Skurzynski

## ACKNOWLEDGMENTS

The author is grateful to the U.S. Postal Service managers, supervisors, and administrators who made this book possible: Linda Modetz at the Coronado Station in Santa Fe; Richard Forslund at the Millcreek branch in Salt Lake City; Rick Cunningham at the Airport Post Office in Salt Lake City; Susan Johnson at the Salt Lake City Main Post Office, Communications Division; and, most of all, at the Salt Lake City Main Post Office, communications manager Beverly Burge, who checked regulations and opened paths time after time.

Thanks, too, go to the postal employees pictured in this book: Louis Sandoval, James Boscon, Michael Wallace, Gerald H. Holt, Ben Lopez, and David Neal; and a warm and special thank-you to letter carrier Cynthia Stewart.

That warmth extends, too, to Karen Mitchell and George Alexander, who aren't pictured in the book but who are always pleasant, capable, and ready to offer help at the Millcreek Post Office.

The five behind-the-scenes photos at Coronado Station were taken by Ted Alm, and Larry Jones assisted the author with the lighting at the Salt Lake City Main Post Office photo sessions.

Bradbury Press
Macmillan Publishing Company
866 Third Avenue
New York, NY 10022

Maxwell Macmillan Canada, Inc.
1200 Eglinton Avenue East
Suite 200
Don Mills, Ontario M3C 3N1

Macmillan Publishing Company is part of the Maxwell Communication Group of Companies.

First edition
Printed and bound in Hong Kong
10 9 8 7 6 5 4 3 2 1

The text of this book is set in 15/25pt Century Old Style.
Design by Beth Tondreau Design

LIBRARY OF CONGRESS CATALOGING-IN-PUBLICATION DATA
Skurzynski, Gloria
   Here comes the mail / by Gloria Skurzynski — 1st ed.
      p.  cm.
   Summary: The inner workings of the postal system are revealed as the author traces the path of a little girl's letter from her home in New Mexico to her cousin's home in Utah. Includes tips on how to address an envelope.
   ISBN 0-02-782916-2
   [1. Postal service—Fiction.]  I. Title
PZ7.S6287He  1992
[E]—dc20                                                          91-40454

*For Stephanie Joan Alm*

*and Katherine Alane Ferguson*

**W**hile Kathy was visiting her cousin Stephanie, Stephanie's mother took a picture of the two girls. The next day, Kathy flew home on an airplane.

Later, Stephanie's mother brought the picture home from the photo shop. "I wish Kathy could see this picture," Stephanie said. "She'd love it."

"Why don't you mail it to her?" her mother suggested. "Here's an envelope the picture will fit in." Stephanie's mother wrote a little note to go with the picture and slipped both inside the envelope. Then she addressed it to Kathy.

"Let me write Kathy's name on it, too," Stephanie said,
"so she'll know it's really from me."

"Want me to spell her name for you?" her mother asked.

"No, I can do it myself." Using a red marker, Stephanie drew a
big heart on the back of the envelope. In dark blue, she printed
a *K* and an *A*. Then a *T*…

She thought for a while and put down an *H*. Then she thought some more.

"Having trouble?" her mother asked.

"I can't remember what comes after the *H*," Stephanie admitted.

"It's a *Y*. Better hurry, honey. The letter carrier will be here any minute."

"Lick this, please, Minnie," Stephanie said, holding a stamp in front of her dog's nose. Minnie was good at licking things. The stamp stuck fast to the right-hand corner of the envelope.

Stephanie ran up the driveway. She knew how to put a letter into the mailbox, then pull up the red flag on the side of the box. The raised flag told the letter carrier to stop and pick up whatever was inside.

But when Stephanie reached the mailbox, it held three letters and a newspaper. The letter carrier had already come. She was too late!

Slowly she scuffed back down the drive-way. "I missed the mailman," she told her mother. "Now I can't mail the picture today."

"Sure you can," her mother said. "We'll stop at the post office when we go to town for groceries."

Their branch post office was in a big, new building. After they drove into the parking lot, Stephanie's mother said, "I'll wait here in the car while you mail the letter."

Once before, Stephanie had gone inside the post office, when she'd sent a birthday card to Grandpa. She remembered exactly how it was done. She pulled the handle to open the slot and dropped the letter into the opening.

On the other side of the wall, the letter landed in a canvas cart called a gurney. All day long, more and more letters fell into that gurney and into another one next to it. By the time the post office closed, the gurneys held a lot of mail.

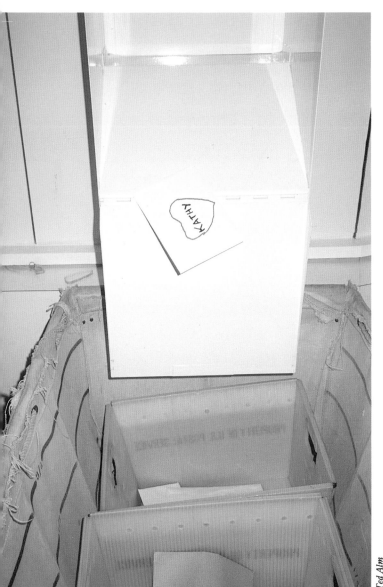

Ted Alm

Ted Alm

Louis and Jim loaded all the mail into a gurney, then wheeled the gurney onto a large truck. As the evening sky grew dusky, Louis drove the truck to a bigger city sixty miles away. That city has a U.S. Postal Service building as big as five football fields put together.

Ted Alm

Ted Alm

There, Postal Service employees work all night long to sort mail and send it on its way. The gurney holding Kathy's letter was rolled up to a big machine. Michael dumped the gurney, dropping all the letters onto a moving conveyor belt.

As the belt swept along, odd-sized envelopes or extra-large envelopes got pulled out and sent in different directions. Only the letter-sized mail moved ahead to one of the "facer-canceler" machines.

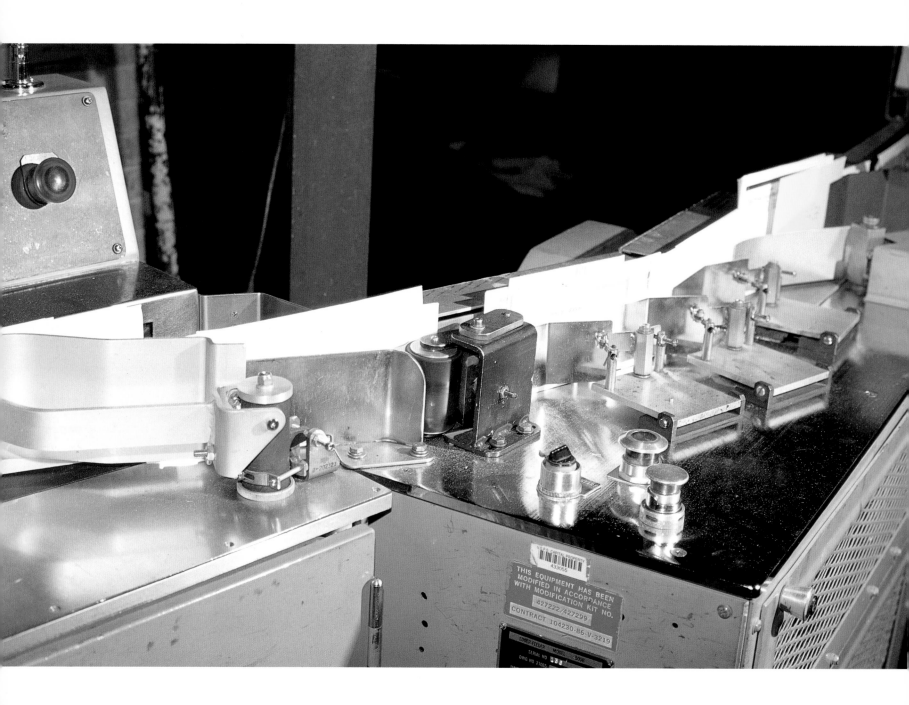

THIS EQUIPMENT HAS BEEN
MODIFIED IN ACCORDANCE
WITH MODIFICATION KIT NO.
427222/427299
CONTRACT 104230-86-V-3219

EDGER-FEEDER    MODEL   500B
SERIAL NO        DWG NO 27066-

108 Coyote Road
Santa Fe, NM 87505

ALBUQUERQUE, NM
PM
8 JUN
1992
87101

WE MEET
THE
CHALLENGE

Kathy Dale
2559 Spring Haven Drive
Salt Lake City, UT 84109-4032

 

    All postage stamps are printed with a special kind of ink. Ultraviolet lights in the facer-canceler machine search for the special ink in stamps. If an envelope has no stamp, it's pushed out of the machine and sent back to the person who mailed it.

    Since the letter to Kathy had a stamp, rubber belts whizzed it past rollers coated with ink. Raised letters on the rollers canceled the stamp and at the same time printed a postmark— the city, state, ZIP code, and the date.

Once Kathy's letter had been postmarked, Gerald put it into a tray with hundreds of other letters. They were carried to a different machine, called the optical character reader—OCR, for short. Ten letters streak through the OCR every single second.

In the OCR, a green band of light reads the street address, city, state, and ZIP code on an envelope—but only if the address has been typed or computer-printed, or hand-printed very neatly in capital letters.

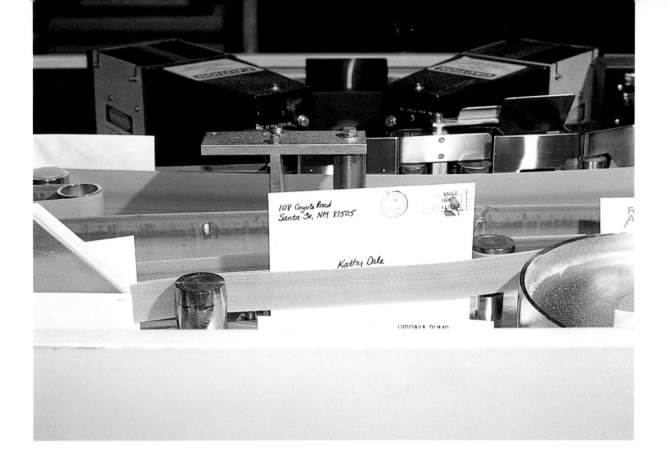

After the OCR reads an address, it sprays a bar code across the bottom of the envelope. A bar code—black lines standing straight up, looking something like a comb with broken teeth—holds information about where a letter is to be delivered.

Since Kathy's address was handwritten, not printed, the OCR couldn't read it, so the letter got pushed out of the OCR machine to be carried to a letter-sorting machine.

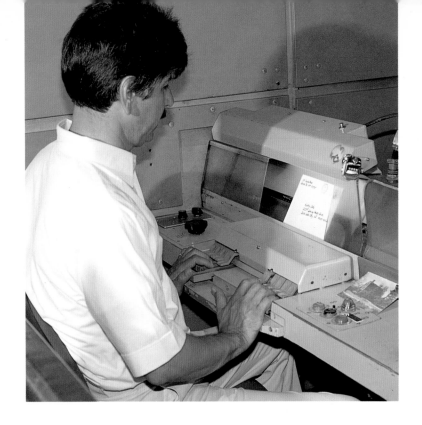

Ben is one of more than a dozen sorters who "key" on the letter-sorting machine. Ben glanced at Kathy's ZIP code and in just one second, keyed (typed) it into his machine. He keyed only the first three numbers of the ZIP code. That's all the machine needed to shoot the letter into a bin with other letters going to the same part of the United States.

Next, Kathy's letter got stacked, bundled, and put into a sack that was thrown onto a gurney. Dave hooked a row of gurneys onto his "mule" and drove them outside to the loading dock. Stars had faded and the sky was beginning to grow light as Dave loaded all the sacks onto a truck. Soon the truck rolled away from the dock, carrying the mail to the airport.

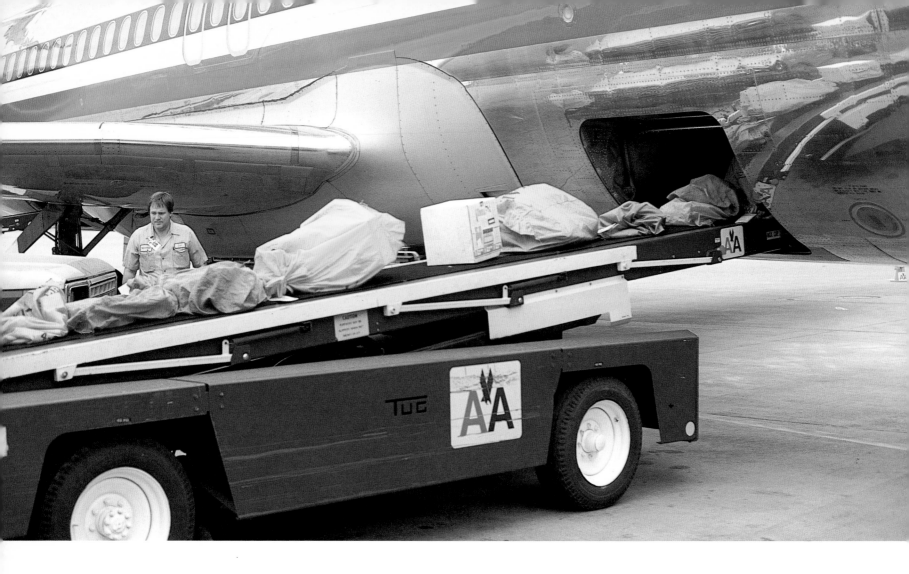

Just after the sun had risen, the sack holding Stephanie's letter to Kathy reached the airport runway. While passengers watched through the airplane windows, brightly colored mail sacks rolled up a ramp and into the plane's cargo bay.

Kathy's letter took longer. Since it had no bar code, it had to be keyed once more on a letter-sorting machine. A postal employee typed the third, fourth, and fifth numbers of the ZIP code, which sent Kathy's letter to a bin marked for the post office nearest her house.

By noon the airplane had landed in the city where Kathy lives. Another truck carried the mail sacks to the city's main post office. It backed up to the dock, where the mail was unloaded and carried inside. A bar-code sorter quickly scanned and sorted all the letters that had bar codes.

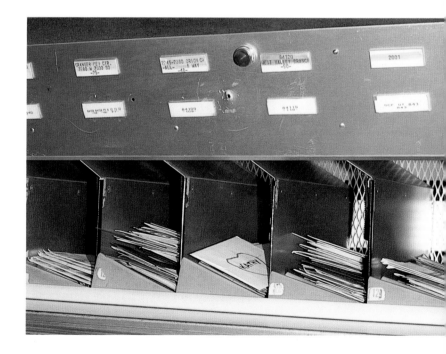

At seven-thirty the following morning, Cindy arrived at the branch post office where she works. Several trays of mail waited for her. She placed the letters, one by one, into separate slots. Every single house or apartment on her delivery route has its own numbered slot at the post office. The letter to Kathy went into a slot marked 2559.

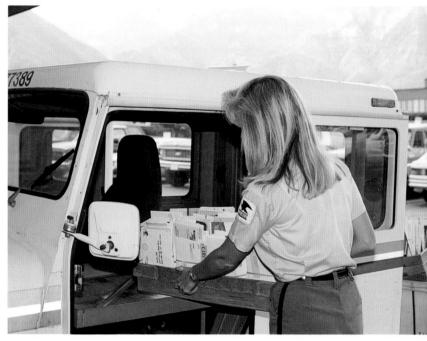

After she'd sorted all her mail and put it back into the trays, Cindy set the trays in a gurney that she wheeled to the parking lot. She loaded the trays into her truck and was ready to deliver the mail.

That afternoon, through her living-room window, Kathy saw the mail truck turn onto her street. Every day, Kathy tries to be at her front door just as the mail arrives. She loves to take the letters out of the mailbox and bring them into the house, even though the mail is hardly ever for her.

This day was different. "Here's a letter for you, Kathy," Cindy called out after she'd pulled her truck to a stop at the curb.

"For me?"

"It has your name on it."

Kathy hurried to the steps as Cindy came to meet her.

When Cindy gave her the letter, Kathy saw K–A–T–H–Y printed inside a large red heart.

Cindy said, "You have such a big smile, I can tell it must be something wonderful."

"Yes! It's from my cousin Stephanie!"

Kathy waved a quick good-bye to Cindy and ran into the house. She opened the envelope, then hurried to find her father and show him the picture.

"Daddy, it really is something wonderful!" she cried.

"What is?" he asked.

"Look!" she said, holding up the picture. "Look what I got in the mail!"

STEPHANIE ALM
108 COYOTE RD
SANTA FE NM  87505-3718

ALBUQUERQUE, NM
PM
8 JUN
1992

WE MEET
THE
CHALLENGE

KATHY DALE
2559 SPRING HAVEN DR
SALT LAKE CITY UT  84109-4032

Bar code

# THE U.S. POSTAL SERVICE WOULD LIKE TO SEE LETTERS ADDRESSED THIS WAY:

If possible, type or computer-print the address, using capital letters. Otherwise, hand-print the address as neatly as possible, using capital letters. Avoid periods and commas.

— Use a complete return address.

Use abbreviations: For ROAD ........................Use RD
                        DRIVE ...........................DR
                        STREET ..........................ST
                        AVENUE .........................AVE
                        APARTMENT ................APT
                        NORTH .........................N
                        EAST .............................E
                        SOUTH..........................S
                        WEST .............................W

Use the two-letter abbreviations for states and the District of Columbia:

| | | | |
|---|---|---|---|
| AL — Alabama | IL — Illinois | MT — Montana | RI — Rhode Island |
| AK— Alaska | IN — Indiana | NE — Nebraska | SC — South Carolina |
| AZ — Arizona | IA — Iowa | NV — Nevada | SD — South Dakota |
| AR— Arkansas | KS — Kansas | NH — New Hampshire | TN — Tennessee |
| CA— California | KY — Kentucky | NJ — New Jersey | TX — Texas |
| CO— Colorado | LA — Louisiana | NM— New Mexico | UT — Utah |
| CT— Connecticut | ME— Maine | NY — New York | VT — Vermont |
| DE— Delaware | MD— Maryland | NC — North Carolina | VA — Virginia |
| DC— District of Columbia | MA— Massachusetts | ND — North Dakota | WA— Washington |
| FL — Florida | MI — Michigan | OH — Ohio | WV— West Virginia |
| GA— Georgia | MN— Minnesota | OK — Oklahoma | WI — Wisconsin |
| HI — Hawaii | MS — Mississippi | OR — Oregon | WY— Wyoming |
| ID — Idaho | MO— Missouri | PA — Pennsylvania | |

Always put the ZIP code on the last line, next to the city and state. If you know the nine-number ZIP code, you should use it. The last four numbers, the ones after the dash, tell the exact part of a city block, or even the particular apartment house, where a letter will be delivered.

If you can't follow all these rules, don't worry. The U.S. Postal Service will still deliver your letter. Addressing envelopes this way, though, makes the mail go faster.